Ethan Long

PRESENTS

FRIGHT CLUB

SCHOLASTIC INC.

ISBN 978-0-545-92769-7

Copyright © 2015 by Ethan Long. All rights reserved.
Published by Scholastic Inc., 557 Broadway, New York, NY 10012,
by arrangement with Bloomsbury Children's Books.
SCHOLASTIC and associated logos are trademarks and/or registered trademarks of Scholastic Inc.

12 11 10 9 8 7 6 5 4 3 2 1   15 16 17 18 19 20/0

Printed in the U.S.A.   08

This edition first printing, September 2015

Artwork created with graphite pencil on Strathmore drawing paper, then scanned and colorized digitally
Book design by Ethan Long and Yelena Safronova
Handlettering by Ethan Long; typeset in Sprocket BT

To all my friends in dark places

It was the night before Halloween when Vladimir
called one last Fright Club meeting to go over
OPERATION KIDDIE SCARE.

Vladimir peered out the peephole.

Awwwwwww, look! An adorable little bunny!

The bunny had no time for small talk.

May I join Fright Club?

What do you want?
My name is Frances Foxx, Public Attorney. My client states that you denied her inclusion in your so-called Fright Club.
Frances W. Foxx

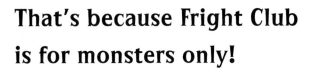

Vladimir tried to refocus.

The monsters definitely had some scary moves,
but not in the way Vladimir had hoped.

BAM! BAM!
BAM!

went the door.

Vladimir slammed the door behind him.

What are we going to do?!?

NOTHING! If you ignore cute little critters, they eventually go away!

But the critters did NOT go away.

Turns out, not only monsters make ghoulish faces,

scary moves,

and chilling sounds.

And when it comes to scaring,
the more the merrier.

So when Halloween arrived, Fright Club was ready.

Vladimir was sure that Operation Kiddie
Scare wouldn't be just good . . .

... it would be SCARY good!